PRIVATE ADMISSION

A Black Comedy

Antonio Robinson

First Edition 2022

ISBN Paperback: 979-8-218-10289-0
ISBN Hardcover: 979-8-218-09913-8
ASIN Ebook: B0BL1Q7WRG
Library of Congress Control Number: 2022920714

Cover design by: Kristen Thorley
Edited by: Bass Jenkins

Antonio Robinson Publishing
Charlotte, NC 28217

PRINTED IN THE UNITED STATES OF AMERICA
1 2 3 4 5 6 7 8 9 0

"The curiously comical aspect of everyday events conceals from us the very real suffering caused by our passions."

Barnave

ALSO BY ANTONIO ROBINSON

The Things We Need

CONTENTS

i.   Meeting The Worker On Glory Road

ii.   The Simp In His Car Beside The Dumpster

iii. Bloody, Officer!

iv.   The Boys In The Woods

v.   In Vino Veritas

vi.   Mirrorcle

vii. Brave Prude World

PRIVATE ADMISSION

CHAPTER I

Meeting The Worker
On Glory Road

"So, this is what I look like now, huh?"

Muffin stared in the mirror in the bathroom of the fast-food restaurant, whose name most people in the world recognize instantly, condemning herself. It had been some time since she'd looked at herself. Not just the occasional glance to make sure she wasn't too hideous; really looked herself in the eyes with a genuine stare. The desire to be more for a man than simply a bedfellow had all but diminished. After several years on the road, their faces had melted into an abstraction of pride, lust, and rage. The three-headed beast from all times. When the emotion was

1

strong enough, she could feel it imprinting into her skin and onto her face. Like cigarette smoke staining the walls in the room of a chain-smoker, her face was stained with the ugliness of men. That same face that she was now staring at, with the overgrown nose hair that jutted out from her left nostril and curled into a question mark (it reminded her of Pinocchio, except the hair didn't extend with lies, but bad choices), repulsed by who she saw.

The door rattled. It was locked. Her eyes darted from the mirror to the door. Whoever was on the other side tried entering again, pushing with more force the second time.

The deadbolt sounded off as it hit the sides of the security plate.

"I really gotta peeeee, mom," a high-pitched voice came from the other side of the door.

Muffin was born in this time in postmodernity. Where deviant obsessions of all kinds rose from the bane of society and stalked the streets in every town and city. They expressed themselves in different ways, but the infatuation remained in focus. And with the public greeting the worst of itself with open arms, expediting its' demise, destruction was more of an expectant than a surprise.

For personal gain, she'd learned to be attentive to the needs of men. Or at least make them forget their needs and concentrate on what they wanted. Glory Road was littered with wants. And she'd found that when men's needs got too hard to fulfill, they'd settle for what they fancied most. When held under the light, both seemed to dazzle just the same.

Muffin was in her late twenties, but you had to add ten years to figure out the age her face looked. Like tree rings telling the weather conditions of each year of that tree's life, the holes in the bend of her elbows and hands, scratches on her arms and legs, and marks under her nose told of what kind of life she'd led. Age only carries meaning for the body; the face is easily manipulated. Women, young and old, will understand this. Men, young and old, will fall victim.

The lone tattoo on her right arm was faded but still noticeable. In its dwindling state, it now served as a reminder of how feelings passed. She wanted to get it removed but had decided against this idea. Its' light was growing dim, she reasoned. It would disappear into nothingness on its own.

She rubbed it now and had a flashback to the thoughtless days which produced the word she'd made permanent to mark those times: YOLO.

You Only Live Once.

It was inked in Fearless Script font. She'd gotten it when she was a teenager. Before she realized how long *Once* could be.

She traveled down to *Forever Young* tattoo shop to immortalize the feeling of being invincible. The irony of feeling indomitable while acknowledging her certain demise only dawned on her when she was older.

Now, just like the mostly faded tattoo, that feeling had waned. And what was left were the bitter pills of an indifferent world she'd never been told of in her youth. Before she'd had to trade the shower across the hall from her childhood for the sink in a fast-food restaurant where strangers exchanged stares for judgment.

This was the bathroom she used to wash up in on most mornings. As long as the staff didn't kick her out. Activity in the restaurant during the early morning was minimal. Most people preferred to go through the drive-thru so they could grab their food and head to work right after. That and traffic in the city had increased tenfold over the past few years. You could easily add 20 minutes onto your commute if you stopped at the wrong time. Breakfast was risky enough without having to go inside.

She worked Glory Road all night; only stopping to freshen up in the 7-eleven at the opposite end. She'd made the trek enough to trust her instincts during the iniquitous hours of the night.

There was a police station at just about the midway point. DCKHED PD (Don't Care Kid Hope Everybody Dies Police Department). That didn't slow any of the activity. They were all just numbers. And those could be manipulated too. Anytime Muffin saw the crows gathered, she knew there was quota to be met. She'd even had a sinking suspicion that they were using the road for training.

The smell in the bathroom was rancid. She could see the bright yellow dried urine stains on the toilet seat in the stall behind her from the mirror. Old pads lay on the dirt-stained tile beside the toilet. The night crew couldn't be bothered to clean the bathrooms. And she didn't blame them. Even civilized adults could be nasty when the doors were closed.

There were repulsive messages, phone numbers for "anyone d.t.f", and other markings written onto the walls in the tiny ladies' room.

Walking in always felt like entering a cave, having to decipher the wall drawings to determine who the individuals were that left the messages behind. In places like this, there would likely be a teenage culprit behind most of what she saw scribbled. Or women like her who came in to freshen up.

"Tis' what it tis', Muff," she said in a low tone. "They don't come to me for eye candy."

Muffin didn't wear much make-up. Electing to go without on most days, whether she was working or not. What did the men care? They weren't paying for a Barbie Doll. To them, she was faceless.

The door rattled again.

"I'll be out in a minute," Muffin said with a hint of aggravation in her voice that she'd meant to hide.

She stared at the door. It rested back into place as though it were sighing.

"Sorry," came an older female voice from the other side.

"I'm gonna pee down my leg if I don't go soon!"

Her daughter. She could tell from the pitch that the child was probably no older than six.

"Shhh. Be patient, honey."

5

Muffin could hear the embarrassment in her voice. She turned her attention back to the mirror; now aware that she'd need to hurry. The next knock would be coming from the staff rushing her out so their paying customers could use the loo.

"But I gotta go!" The child exclaimed.

The staff knew who she was and what profession she'd chosen for herself. Like a lot of employees at fast food restaurants, they were young. High School age kids mostly. At the age where responsibility was nil and the judgment towards those with responsibilities was lofty. A mixture of 40-something-year-old men and women who resented working next to the younger generation filled out the cast for the vaudeville show. A cast who'd soon be replaced by A.I. Or so they seemed to always be threatening on the news to a mostly uninterested public who were already drowning in debt.

Muffin accepted their looks when she came inside to bathe in the morning. Their time would come. A couple of the boys would eventually become her customers. The women, her peers on the road. The next generation of addicts and deviant workers. The circle of trife.

She pulled a pack of wet wipes out of the small, burgundy flower-patterned purse she kept with her, snatched out two wipes, and gave herself a once over with them. She combed out her wig and stopped to look at the nose hair.

Should I pluck it out?

PRIVATE ADMISSION

No. With any luck, it'd curl long enough to strangle her with bad decisions. A first. She left the bathroom shortly thereafter.

When she opened the door, she locked eyes with the little girl (and if she didn't have pee running down her leg already, she might have with the fear Muffin saw in her eyes) who stepped back towards her mom, shocked by Muffin's appearance. She could feel the little's girl's eyes staring at the nose hair. The child wiped her nose almost squeamish.

The woman, middle-aged, looked to Muffin like a live-action Velma(she even had thick, black frame glasses).

She stared at Muffin with a raised eyebrow, shielding her innocent like a swan shields its' cygnet.

This isn't airborne, honey. The mother expressed with her protection.

Muffin stepped aside so they could enter the ladies' room.

They reluctantly stepped towards the door; excepting Muffin's gesture though they couldn't hide the disdain on their faces. Fear might be a better word. Most folks aren't ready to come face to face with those that are used for fodder in the news.

Muffin walked towards the exit.

In sync, mother and daughter stuck their heads out to catch one last glance at what stumbled out of the bathroom.

⚢ ⚢ ⚢

7

Antonio Robinson

I Can See It In Your Eyes
Behind That Smile The Devil Lies

Rachel strummed a sour, off-melody note on her untuned, battered brown guitar as she belted the notes to her original tune. The guitar was covered in peace stickers and other stickers that suggested Rachel had traveled at some point in her life.

She walked up and down Glory Road playing that guitar every day. She'd arrive with the heat from the morning sun and left with the cool touch from the moonlight. Her hair started to turn salt and pepper and her steps grew more labored after years of ambling to and fro; seeking whoever needed company for a spell. Rachel stopped climbing into the passenger seat of the strange men lurking in the area. Her role was now the Albatross on the road. Many knew her and the ugly tunes she strummed, but most paid the old bird no mind.

Her clothes were the same. Worn, patchy, and big. Blue jeans and a white shirt with the phrase *Jesus Loves You* (the Je was faded so you could only make out sus Loves You from afar), and black slide-in shoes were her usual attire. Her skin had turned dry and scaly from years in the bare sun. There were warts in patches on her face and neck that could be mistaken for freckles. One lone wart stood out prominent on her right cheek. She might've tried to doll it up in her prime, but its appearance now seemed only to look like pieces of her were trying to escape; like a parasite fleeing from its' dying host.

Once every few months the cops would respond to a call from someone who spotted her on the main highway. She liked to walk the streets in the bare on occasion. But even this had become a normal sighting. They picked her up more as a formality. They knew she'd be back on Glory Road.

Watching her stand near where the Johns picked their partners, her guitar now sounded like the call of a rooster in the neighborhood of a suburban town it shouldn't be in. The signal for the start of a new day.

Just then a cherry red, 92' Toyota Camry halted at the spot where he'd picked up his partner. The paint on the car had oxidized through the years. The man hopped out white hot. He locked eyes with Muffin as he walked around to the passenger side and turned his attention back to the matter at hand. She noted how cartoonish the entire incident was unfolding.

Muffin spotted the worker through the window. They caught each other's eye just as the man threw the car door open.

"Ah-"

He gripped the worker's throat, catching her scream before it reached its crescendo. Her neck was pinched between his semi-closed fist as though he were trying to juice an orange.

Rachel stopped playing her guitar. Her final strum rang out as though she was sounding the alarm for the workers.

She and Muffin waited to see how far the encounter would go. Neither would break it up or even call out for help. The attention wasn't worth the hassle. Besides, there was no need to be included among the deceased for the transgressions of a stranger. This tale was as old as the profession itself. They watched.

"Give it back you rotten-crotched thief," the man said with a tone that meant the worker knew what he was referring to.

She grabbed his wrist.

"Le- g-," she managed as she gasped for what little air she could suck down her windpipes.

His grip loosened but remained firm enough so that she understood he was still in control of how this encounter would unfold.

"Give it back!"

Her right hand dropped from his wrist to her right pocket. She pulled out $200 and held it towards the man to take.

He snatched it with his free hand and eyeballed it. He balled the money up in his fist, snatched her out of his car, and threw her onto the road. The contents of her purse spilled out onto the pavement beside her.

PRIVATE ADMISSION

He hopped in his car and drove off without looking at any of the women. His car sped down the road as he floored the pedal.

The woman sat on the ground watching her John disappear down the road.

"You could have did something," she said switching her attention to Muffin. "What kinda woman watches another woman get handled like that by a man?"

"Girl, shut up. I watched a thief get caught. That's about as much as I care to do," Muffin said and waited. "Be careful who you steal from. They won't all bring you back."

"Why should I listen to you? You're out here with me."

Muffin didn't care if she listened or not. She began strolling further down Glory Road. Women like her didn't survive long. Hard to get attached to someone that doesn't have a sense of self-preservation.

"Your nose hair is curly," the woman said watching Muffin disappear down the road.

Rachel strummed her guitar.

The woman began gathering her things into her purse.

Muffin continued towards her own troubles.

CHAPTER II

The Simp In His Car
Beside The Dumpster

"I can feel the cancer eating away at my body."

Jimmee sat in his car listening to the hobo commit to his story before asking for a financial contribution to his morning till. A dance as familial as the electric slide.

The top of his head was bare and the hair on the side, still mostly black, was grown wild. It'd probably been a few years since he'd gotten a decent shave. He wore baggy blue jeans, a black hoodie, and filthy white socks with slides. The right slide was held together with duct tape.

PRIVATE ADMISSION

In the cool morning breeze, Jimmee caught the smell of must drifting from the man. In his head, he wrinkled his nose when the smell wafted into his nostrils, but talking to the man, he kept a straight face.

"Every day. People mosey on by. And we all got our own problems and don't no man owe me nothing. But I can feel the cancer eating at my *body*," the hobo said and emphasized body when he spoke. "And I know this must be my punishment for what I done did. Karma, if you believe in that sort of thing. But to them, the regular folk working their jobs and them corporate folk pushing all the buttons, I'm an idea. Not a man," the hobo said and pointed his index finger to the sky and brought it down slowly in the direction of Glory Road.

A police siren blared. A moment later the squad car zoomed by.

"And to the DCK's, I'm just a paycheck," he said and followed the squad car with his finger until he no longer could.

Jimmee rolled the window further down in his cream-white, 06' PT Cruiser. The button was on the center console. He slid it down without having to turn away from the hobo.

He'd seen the man a couple of times a week when he parked near the dumpster beside the 7-eleven. Most times they opted to speak with only a nod, but they shared words on occasion.

"You see that?" The hobo asked pointing at nothing in general.

Jimmee looked in the direction he was pointing. The sun was out, and traffic was moving, but nothing special. He turned his attention back to the hobo.

"What?" Jimmee asked and turned back in the direction he was pointing.

"*That's* my t.v.," he responded; his voice boomed for emphasis. "That's what I look at day in and day out. When the lights is on, I see working-class folk, kids going to school, and people out trying to get their fix. Everybody moving around like ants before the winter," he said eyeing Jimmee with an understanding they both silently agreed on. "But at night, the world look different. Or really the world look the same, but people act different. The dark brings out the darkness in men. Even the darkness can't hold all that ugliness though. They two different things."

Jimmee pondered the man's ramblings. All hobos had these types of stories. All of them. Fragmented puzzles that may or may not mean anything at all. Poverty created more intellectuals than Universities ever could. He'd seen men and women claim a supreme understanding of the true meanings of life and still more claim they were God himself. Men who sat around all day with nothing to do but think came up with all kinds of stories and harebrained schemes that needn't be true to anyone but themselves. He surmised that every city had its own Plato sleeping under the bridge.

"You get that beer money yet?"

PRIVATE ADMISSION

Jimmee looked towards the dumpster and spotted one of the workers from the road. Her pink spaghetti-strap shirt had a brown stain on the front and her white denim skirt looked a little too big. Or even more true, it had once fit before her vices got the best of her. He could see a shoestring tied through the loops to hold it up.

"Gimme a minute, honey," the hobo said and turned his attention back to Jimmee. "Hey, fella. You got $2.43 to spare?"

"Exact change and all, huh?" Jimmee said sarcastically. He pulled three dollars out of his wallet in the center console and handed it to the man. He didn't make it a point to hand out money, especially since he'd seen the man on multiple occasions (because just like stray animals, men and women with close to nothing always come back to a provider), but he parted ways with a few bucks.

"Get your thrills, old man," Jimmee said and looked towards the dumpster.

He wasn't sure if the hobo was old or not. A hard life does that. Hard drugs and drink too. Hard lies even. Truthfully, they could've been the same age. Another thirty-something male determined to make the problems of the world his own. Forgetting that in postmodern society and on the sunny side of the dirt, the goal was to establish oneself under the agreed laws of the land, without losing your life or your mind. Though the hobo was still alive, the world had gotten the best of his mind.

Get Your Thrills, Old Man.

Jimmee watched him hold the dollar bills up to the sun as though he were checking their authenticity.

"Look good to me," he said playfully. "Appreciate it fella. Be safe out here. And if you can't do that, name it after me," the hobo said while gathering his things into an old shopping cart. There were cans, old clothes, a broom, and other things he'd collected from the side of the road and around town in the shopping cart.

Jimmee watched him scurry over to the dumpster and pass the money to the worker so she could get their morning medicine from the gas station.

☿ ☿ ☿

The radio played the same ten songs. Nothing could escape the monotony of what popular entertainment had degenerated into. Crime and sex. Art, and the expressions that it inspired, had become formulaic. Artists turned pied pipers to exploit the naive sensibilities of an ever-changing child audience. And either by design or from a lack of wit, the artist had turned from milkmaid of the people to con artist with no moral compass who played stand-in for the true artisans that realized the First Amendment needn't be exploited but utilized to adva-

"Why you got that dumb look on your face?"

Her words smacked Jimmee out of his thoughts. He looked at Muffin who'd gotten a little too close while he was stuck in his train of thought. Something he was beginning to do more of than anything worth doing. A trait he hated, but found he couldn't shake it.

"No Reason," Jimmee said trying not to sound surprised.

"You daydreaming this early in the morning, dude?" Muffin asked and began to laugh.

"I guess so. Not much else happening round here right now. Where you coming from?"

Muffin pointed towards Glory Road.

"The road."

Jimmee looked in the direction of the road.

The hobo and his worker had vanished half an hour ago or so. He could make out another worker making her trek down the road in the distance. She reminded him of one of the undead in the Romero movies. Except these undead meant to drain your essence in other ways.

"Anything lively happening further up?"

"No. Nothing out of the ordinary I mean. Chick got tossed out a car a little bit ago."

"Tossed out? For what?"

"She stole some money, officer," Muffin responded while she was surveying the gas station and the surrounding area. There were none of her customers in sight. Only customers for the 7-eleven. "You got any more questions? Or should I have an attorney present?" She said turning her attention back to Jimmee.

"You gon' get inside?"

Muffin gave the station and the road another once over before walking around to the passenger side of the Cruiser.

"Why you always out here Jimmee?" Muffin asked as she settled into the seat. She adjusted it all the way back to stretch her 5'9" frame. "And why'd you buy such a small car?" She said resting her head back and closing her eyes. She'd taken a nap in his car a handful of times. Jimmee didn't want anything from her. Nothing tangible anyway. But she wouldn't call what she felt when she was around Jimmee as feeling "safe". But in contrast to the type of men she encountered on a daily basis, he was tame.

"I got swindled by a crooked salesman at an auction. That's why. Guy sold me a lemon the first time and when I brought it back for a refund, he swapped cars instead. Crooked cat. But that's any good salesman. This is what I got in the trade. Learned one lesson though."

"Oh, really? Humor me. What did you learn?" Muffin asked only half-interested in his response. She didn't understand cars or what people discussed to buy them. She went by the sight test. If it looked good, she liked it.

"Never buy a used car without taking it to a mechanic first. And if you know one, that's even better. But make sure you take it to a professional before settling."

"You're sweet, Jim," Muffin said and tapped his cheek before resting her palm on his jawline and glancing at him with a look more of pity than admiration. Just then he sounded like most of the suckers she ran into every day on the road. "Good for you," she said and rested her hand on her thigh.

18

PRIVATE ADMISSION

Jimmee pulled his composition book from the holder on the door and began writing something down.

Muffin, who had closed her eyes again, opened them as the sound of Jimmee's pen scribbling into his notebook warranted her attention.

"You still trying to write that book?" Muffin asked as she watched him with feigning interest.

Jimmee remained quiet for a moment and finished up the line he was working on.

"You can't try to do something. You either do it or you don't," Jimmee said looking up from his notebook.

"What's failure then?"

"Failure depends on who made the rules," Jimmee said and by the look on Muffin's face, he was satisfied with his response.

"That sounds good," she said not wanting to fall further down the rabbit hole. "Finding whatever inspiration you looking for?"

If by inspiration she meant excepting the status quo and trying to find a way to exploit it, then yes, he'd found exactly what he was looking for.

"One of your nose hairs is curling up. Haven't seen one do that before. New style?" Jimmee said wanting to move on from the current conversation. Like most creative people, he was sensitive about his creation. Especially while he was still in the discovery process. He hadn't gleaned much from Glory Road yet. Truthfully, he'd been waiting on a catastrophe of some kind to occur so he could tell the tale of life in the slums. Apology art was on the rise. Everybody enjoys a glimpse into a life they'll never experience.

Popular literature was cluttered with Young Adult authors and Social Media Influencers. Seems the brands figured that was the easiest way to manipulate the adults out of their wages. Children *are* our future. If only because they're being exploited to fund it.

Postmodernism was all about desire. Glory Road was his muse.

"You wanna pull it out for me?" Muffin asked as she flipped the sun visor and studied her face in the mirror.

"Trim your own fur, Bigfoot."

She side-eyed him.

"Don't get cute," she said and returned to examining herself.

Jimmy watched as she began fixing her wig. She pulled it on either side before settling on its' position and used her fingers to comb it out of her face.

"You're wasting your time with that book, ya know," Muffin said matter of factly.

"And you're wasting your time with that wig," he said offended by her comment. "What'chu mean by that?"

"First," she said and flipped him the bird for his comment about her wig. "Second, women aren't interested in that sorta thing," she responded.

"I don't understand. Women aren't interested in what sorta thing? Words?"

PRIVATE ADMISSION

He'd never asked her opinion of his writing, let alone what she felt other people thought about books in general. He understood that half of the population was illiterate (at least according to studies from people he'd never heard of), but he knew even the unlearned appreciated a good yarn. Metaphors be damned.

"No. That's not what I mean. You don't do anything."

Jimmee had heard this sentiment before. His mind always went back to a quote he learned during his acting classes in college, "Action is character. What a person does is what he is, not what he says," compliments of Syd Field.

And wasn't waiting for something interesting to happen *doing* something?

He glanced over at Muffin who was still fixated on herself in the small visor mirror. She pulled the pack of wet wipes from her purse and snatched one free. She wiped the sides of her nose, and underneath her eyes, and tossed the used wipe out of the window.

"You don't wanna roll these windows up and cut the air on? It's starting to get hot out here."

"Can't. AC don't work," Jimmee responded and held back a smile. Only women could casually utter scathing remarks about other people's lives and still make demands.

She popped the visor back into place.

"Jim, you're dow-"

Muffin began but was interrupted by two taps on her door. Startled, she turned towards the window.

Jimmee saw the DCKHED's badge and then the officer leaning into the window. He could tell the officer was taking a mental assessment of the situation.

"How y'all doing today?" The DCK asked with a drawl.

"All good."

Jimmy was short. He was parked in an area trafficked by Muffin, the hobo, and those like them.

"That's good. Well, I'm gon' be blunt. This is a hotspot over here and seeing two people hanging out by a dumpster usually isn't a good sign if ya know what I mean," he said and looked directly at Muffin who focused her eyes on her lap and then over at Jimmee. "Understand what I'm getting at?" He asked Jimmee rhetorically. "Lot of trouble happens in this area."

DCKHED tactic. He was fishing. They *were* sitting in a hotspot, but that didn't mean much. Given the current state of affairs in the world, stepping out of one's home could put you in a hotspot of some kind. These officers chose to hang out amongst those who couldn't control themselves. Then lock them up and put them right back on the street. No rehab. No education. No real plans at all. Just to stack charges to justify a complex more complicated than the Riemann Hypothesis. Catch and release. He was fishing in the community cesspool.

"Are you looking for someone?" Jimmee asked trying to hurry along the interaction.

"No. Just making sure I know who's who in my area," the officer responded and stared Jimmee down. "You two stay out of trouble, okay?"

"Sure thing, DCKHED," Jimmee responded.

With that, the officer stood and walked around to the front of the gas station. They had a security guard in the store at least three times a week. Sometimes it'd be a cop from the local station, other times the guard looked like a guy who might've been on his couch just a week prior. Law enforcement was laughable. Seems the only requirement for a badge and a gun was a heartbeat.

"That's my cue," Muffin said. "I'm bout to go play the lotto for a couple hours. You plan to be here all day?"

"I'm gonna head to the park in a few. Sit with the boys for a while. But I'll come back to the road after that," Jimmee responded.

"Well, I'll see you if you're around when I'm done playing the numbers," Muffin said and climbed out of the car.

He watched as she vanished around the side of the gas station.

A worker that Jimmee hadn't noticed appeared from beside the dumpster just as a car pulled in beside Jimmee's Cruiser. She was younger than most of the women on the strip. She had on thong-toe sandals and a deep purple mini-dress. The man nodded towards her and she put on her best attractive walk, sauntered over, and climbed in the passenger seat of her new customer's car.

23

Jimmee watched as they discussed the details of the transaction. He couldn't hear what was being said, but that was the protocol when picking up strange bedfellows.

He could tell by the way the man smiled that they both agreed on the terms. The man pulled off shortly after.

Jimmee opened his notebook and began writing.

CHAPTER III

Bloody, Officer!

With her guitar slung across her back like an old swordsman searching for one last battle, Rachel ambled by the precinct on Glory Road.

The parking lot was filled with squad cars. It wasn't a large building. Made of brick, it used to be an old AME church. The stained glass panes in the window remained to tell the tales of old, southern preachers spitting fire and brimstone to those participants of the now daily debauchery on Glory Road.

DCKHED PD was presented in big black letters on the front of the building. The letters were blue and they stood out grandly against the bright red brick.

WE THE UNWILLING
LED BY THE UNQUALIFIED

Antonio Robinson

TO KILL THE UNFORTUNATE
DIE FOR THE UNGRATEFUL

George snapped his silver zippo lighter shut and ran his thumb along the engraving. It'd been two years since he'd smoked his last cigarette, but the lighter was a gift from his dad so he kept it with him. Didn't help the urges he'd get every so often to spark up a bogey, especially in his line of work, but he'd gotten to the point where he could control his vice. He flipped the top and struck a flame. The flame danced on the tip of the wick before he snapped the lid shut, stifling it. He looked over at his partner, Christopher; a young man, clean-cut, with a look of naivety in his eyes that George remembered all too well from when he'd started twenty years prior. Same wide-eyed look most rookies came into the job with. Over time, that look would be snuffed out. Like the flame from his zippo.

"It's about patience, Chris. We are the hunters. Our job is to bring balance to the people in this city. There are two types of predators out here: Apex One and Apex Two. Apex Two prey on everything below them. Women, children, the elderly, businesses, they don't care. Just a pack of lazy nothings taking whatever they can get. We are Apex One, Chris. They are our targets," George said.

Christopher stared at his partner. He'd barely made it onto the force. His father had been a decorated officer so the Captain passed him as a favor. He never saw any real talent in Christopher and wasn't shy about letting him know.

But sometimes favors are better than talent. And nepotism reigns over all.

"Christopher, sir," he said and watched as George raised his eyebrow. Only his mother called him Chris. He'd never suggested the abbreviation to anyone at the station.

"What?" George asked.

"You called me Chris. My name is Christopher. Sir."

George broke eye contact and rested back in his seat.

Christopher sensed George was in deeper thought than he intended in correcting his Superior.

"Chris is easier," George said finally. "Rolls off the tongue better. Don't be so tight."

George nodded in agreement at his conclusion.

Truthfully, Christopher admired George. His years on the street had to count for something. Besides, it was too early in the day to kick up dust over frivolous issues. He dropped it. If only to keep the peace.

Christopher turned his attention from George to the local news van passing by the station. He read the logo as it drove slowly by.

IF IT BLEEDS IT LEADS NEWS 9!

The station made sure one of their vans was nearby. Always hoping to catch action akin to 10/26/1881. But any excitement would do. Something for the unsuspecting locals to fall asleep to at night.

"Can one of y'all help me with bus fare?"

27

A man, dressed in brown khakis and a collared-red shirt, knocked on Christopher's window startling the two officers. They both looked at the man who seemed to be in genuine distress.

George rolled down Christopher's window from his side.

"What did you say?" George asked as the window finished rolling down.

Christopher studied the man but didn't say anything. His clothing was clean and ironed.

"Bus fare. Can one of you help me out? I got a job interview today, but I don't got enough to make it to the side of town I need to be on for the interview," the man said looking at the two men. "I just need enough to get on the bus."

George studied the man.

"Look, it's $2.20. If I didn't need it, I wouldn't ask, but I'm hard up and I'm trying to get to some money," the man finished pleading his case.

George had been working the streets long enough and had seen a decent amount of fiends bold enough to ask the cops for help with their fix. They made up all kinds of tales about why they needed money. But this man didn't seem like one of them. George pulled his wallet out and snatched $10 from it. He passed the money to the man who grabbed it as it passed in front of Christopher's face.

"Thanks, bro," the man said.

PRIVATE ADMISSION

"Just make sure you get that job, son," George said and gave a firm nod and stare akin to a parent telling his child to behave in school.

The man waived off the two officers and left the parking lot.

"You don't think he'll use that for other things," Christopher said making a hint.

"Maybe. But you can't be skeptical of everybody. Out here, the wolves and the sheep look the same. Until you give em' a reason to bare their teeth."

With that, George cranked up the squad car and pulled out of the station.

♂ ♂ ♂

"So you called us down here because they put salt on your fries?"

A few bystanders stopped to listen in on the conversation between the cops and the irate gentleman. They'd managed to escort him out of the establishment. Not before he hurled more curse words at the staff (and a few of his cold fries).

"That's exactly why I called you down here, officer. These half-wits are trying to kill me."

"So you cussed and tore up that restaurant because of salt on your fries?"

"Yep. I specifically asked them for no salt. They didn't even cook new fries. I have an issue with my blood pressure. I coulda died! Those kids tried to kill me!" The man shouted these last remarks.

"Okay, calm down sir," George said.

Christopher didn't say anything. He only listened to the two converse. He looked around the parking lot. All eyes were trained on the situation.

There was a lot of hand-to-hand action across the street. The officer's presence slowed sales. They wanted them gone probably as much as neither officer wanted to be there. They'd had to find a way to co-exist with one another.

"Whatchu mean calm down!? Are you deaf? Them dummies coulda killed me!"

"Alright, sir," Christopher said turning his attention back to the men. "There's no need to upset yourself any further. I'm sure they made an honest mistake. First job for most of em'. Might be their first week."

"I'm lucky to be yelling at all. I. Coulda. Died!" He repeated his aggression.

"Mannnn! Go home! Leave them DCKHED's alone!"

A man yelled from across the street; unhappy about losing sales, he was trying to rush along the forced presence of his persecutors.

Christopher put a hand up signaling for the men to cease any interference.

"Okay, sir. Let's try and wrap this up. What would you like us to do?" George asked.

"I want you to arrest them."

"Arrest who? The staff? For what exactly?" George asked.

30

PRIVATE ADMISSION

"Attempted murder. Gross negligence. You guys find reasons all the time. Find *something*. Those kids tried to kill me!" The man shouted once again.

George and Christopher looked at each other simultaneously. Neither said a word. They turned their attention back to the man.

"Sir. I think you're just going to have to count your lucky stars and go get you a salad. There's nothing illegal about making a mistake," George said.

"But I'm a taxpayer. You work for me and I order you to do your job!"

Christopher and George looked at each once again. They looked back at the man whose gaze was shifting between the both of them.

"You guys waiting on an invitation?" He asked.

"I'm going to have to ask you to leave the premises," George said.

"What?"

"Leave or I'll arrest you for trespassing."

"But-"

"Get in your car and leave, sir!" George, growing aggravated, was sterner.

Everything got quiet.

The man could tell he was fighting a losing battle. Or at least one that was quickly turning against him.

Christopher tried to think if what George was saying was true, but couldn't remember. He never read any of the handbooks or studied for the test during the academy. He'd winged the whole mess.

The man looked at both officers, indignantly. He stepped between them and stomped to his truck.

"Sometimes you gotta save people from themselves, Chris. He's probably one of those yuppie vegans. Eating cauliflower buffalo wings and drinking root pee," George said.

"Tea, sir," Christopher corrected him.

"What?"

"Root tea. You boil the roots and make tea. I think."

"Whatever, Chris. As long as that yuppie gets in his truck and up the road," George said.

Christopher watched absentmindedly as the man climbed into his truck.

"It's Christopher, sir," he said just out of earshot of George who had turned to enter the restaurant.

"Gonna grab a cup of coffee and a medium fry. With salt," he said and watched the truck back out of its parking space. "Lots of it. You want anything?"

"No. Nothing for me, thanks."

"Suit yourself," George said and entered the restaurant.

Christopher wasn't sure if the man was an Apex Two Predator or not. He looked across the street at the men who, while still alert to their presence, had gone back to business as usual. At that moment, the gentleman in the truck seemed to pose more of a threat.

PRIVATE ADMISSION

Just then an *IF IT BLEEDS IT LEADS NEWS 9!* van pulled into the parking lot. Christopher watched as it pulled up right next to him. The passenger side window rolled down and a microphone was stuck out of the window.

"Care to tell the people what happened?"

"No. Nothing happened," Christopher said fanning away the microphone.

"We just got word that the DCK's got into another near-deadly confrontation with one of our local citizens. To that, you say what?" The reporter asked while shoving the microphone back into Christopher's face.

George walked out of the restaurant before he could answer.

"Looks like the grim reapers are out already. A step too slow today boys. The real action dispersed a little while ago. Just a man-child mad he didn't get his way. Nothing else to see here ladies. Why don't you all just pull on out. I'm sure something more promising is on the horizon."

He'd been handling the news team for some time. Christopher was impressed.

The cameraman, who was driving, and the reporter just stared at George. Both wanted to retort with some witty comeback, but he'd gotten the better of them. The reporter slowly pulled the microphone inside the news van.

George knew it from their silence that he'd gotten the best of them. And there really was nothing to report on at the moment.

"Fine old man. But we'll be close behind. You're bound to slip. Your kind always do."

And with that, the reporter rolled up his window and the news van pulled out of the parking lot.

"Death chasers. Nothing more than a bunch of vultures," George said before turning his attention back to Christopher. "Hop in. I just heard there's something happening further down the road at the gas station."

They both climbed into the squad car and George sped away.

♂ ♀ ♂

"Drop the knife!!"

A knife-wielding civilian was at a stand-off with the police. People had long since stopped pumping their gas to watch the action.

An old catholic woman made the sign of the cross and kissed her Rosary Beads.

George was on one side and Christopher on the other. The man stood in between the two officers shifting his gaze and the knife between the two.

"What's your name?" George asked as he showed the man his palms.

"Squirrel," the man said backing away slowly.

Looking at the man, Christopher could tell the nickname had come from his small stature.

"How old are you Squirrel?"

"30. But what does that have to do with anything?"

PRIVATE ADMISSION

"What's a young guy like you doing out looking to throw the rest of his life away? I'm sure we can figure a way to make sure everybody walks away."

George was being tactical. Christopher caught the vibe and went with it. Maybe he could subdue the man once George got him to let his guard down. He waited for his opportunity.

"You don't know nothing about me. And don't pretend like you care. I see your partner over there. Nervous chump with his hand on his gun," Squirrel said and glanced at Christopher and then down at his hand that *was* on his gun.

"We're cool, Squirrel. Focus on me," George said. "I'm in charge of this outfit. Nobody's gonna do anything without my say so." He said and gave Christopher a look to confirm.

Christopher nodded and slowly moved his hand away from his gun.

Squirrel looked back up at Christopher and then over at George.

"Talk to me, son. What's wrong?"

"I-"

Christopher jumped him, throwing Squirrel to the ground. The crowd at the pumps gasped.

"Savages!!" The old woman screamed.

George, surprised, watched as his partner wrestled on the ground with the man. Snapping to, he searched for the knife, but couldn't find it with his eyes.

Christopher was straddling the man, trying to subdue him on the ground. Just then he looked to George like he was riding one of those mechanical bulls that they have in some bars. The man was trying to buck Christopher off of him but couldn't.

"Drop the knife!" Christopher's voice echoed through the gas station. Everyone watched in horror.

"Get off of me!!! I can't breathe!!!"

They continued to wrestle.

George began strafing around the two men but didn't get down to intervene. He drew his gun which drew more gasps from the crowd that was growing increasingly larger as the tension continued mounting.

"Drop the knife!" George shouted.

"I can't breathe!!" Squirrel repeated.

"Get off of him you savages!!" The old woman shouted. "You're killing him!!"

The situation was headed downhill. George looked over at the old woman and then back down at the two men scuffling on the ground.

Christopher was able to pull Squirrel's hidden arm from underneath him. He was not holding the knife.

George jumped into action and grabbed the man's other arm and, together, they were able to pull him to his feet. Once he'd been lifted, they saw the knife resting flat underneath him.

He gave Christopher a look to acknowledge the dangerous situation he'd put himself in.

PRIVATE ADMISSION

"Grab the knife. I'm gonna put him in the back of the squad car," George said.

Christopher bent to pick up the knife. Just before he picked it up he looked around the gas station at everyone now staring at him. Most had dispersed as the action was over, but some remained to give scathing looks to the officers.

The old woman stood staring and, once again, made the sign of the cross and kissed her Rosary Beads. She mouthed the word *SAVAGES*, turned, and hopped in her gold 1990 Ford Tempo.

Christopher picked up the knife and climbed into the squad car.

George sat in silence for a moment; not even looking in Christopher's direction.

Squirrel had regained some of his composure. Handcuffs and a cage does that to folks.

"That was a stupid thing you did just now, Chris. Got lucky News 9 ain't made their way up here yet. Looks like a few people were shaken up, but nothing serious. You gotta be careful. I don't plan on making no calls home because you felt like John Wayne, cowboy."

Christopher couldn't, or wouldn't utter a retort. George was right and he knew it. His head sunk into his chest.

"Can we stop at Burger King before y'all take me in?" Squirrel leaned forward and directed his question at both officers.

George banged on the plexiglass divider.

Antonio Robinson

"Sit back, Rocky."

Squirrel did as he was told.

George pulled off, slowly, headed towards DCKHED PD to drop off their newly captured prize.

CHAPTER IV

The Boys In The Woods

"You heard bout that rapper that got killed the other day?"

Jimmee was sitting with Forest and Puffy at the park. Forest was in his late 40s and worked a job at a hotel shuttling guests back and forth from the airport. He was still wearing his uniform; a light green collard shirt and brown khakis. And that wasn't his real name. Forest. But he reminded Jimmee of Forest Whitaker so he called him that and, after a while, it stuck. Puffy was a heavyset 40-something man who had a habit of rambling once he was full of his vices. There was no way of telling what he actually did for a living because he talked in hustle. Over time, Jimmee learned that this meant he constantly had a new idea on how to hit a lick or get rich quick. But day in and day out, he wound up back at the table. Launching an unlimited amount of rocks at the sun.

Jimmee had been coming to the park for the past few weeks and had made nice with the men and the others who lurked in and out of the park throughout the day.

It was the afternoon and foot traffic was light. They were sitting on one of two run-down picnic tables underneath the gazebo in the middle of the park. A lone pack of off-brand playing cards sat in the middle of the men. They used them to play Tunk when things were especially boring. When there were enough people, they'd play Spades occasionally. The park was located downhill from the entrance. Not a sharp downhill slope, but you'd need to hike uphill to make it back to the entrance. That small slope gave a bit of added coverage for the illicit activity that took place. There was a water fountain between the entrance and the place where the three men were now seated.

Behind where they were seated was a path that led to a field where children and adults would go to play soccer, frisbee, or to let their dogs roam for a while. During the summer months, folks from the neighborhood could be found sunbathing in the middle of the field as well.

On either side of that path and surrounding the open field were woods. There were old beer bottles, chip bags, and a lot of overall pollution that suggested people frequented the woods. There were tents purposely hidden from the common eye, but if you stared hard enough, you could make out that there was a community of people living in those woods.

"Yup. Them young boys getting all the smoke they looking for right now. Ain't nobody fighting no more. They shooting to kill," Puffy remarked while sanitizing his hands.

Jimmee noticed that about him after spending some time at the park. Puffy was not a small man. 6'5" and roughly 260 pounds. He was friendly enough, but you wouldn't know if he didn't know you. He kept a scowl on his face for the most part. The type of man you wouldn't ask for the time of day even if his watch was digital. But he sanitized his hands often and cleaned up his immediate area of trash no matter whose it was. He had his shortcomings, but he kept it together. Sometimes that mattered more than the addiction. How well you could hold it together. The brain is funny that way.

"Yeah, man. Them young boys better get a grip. Too many people starving out here. All that extra money they like flashing on the live streams like the minions ain't watching. It's like dangling a steak in front of starving wolves," Puffy said.

"They crazy man. Get all that money and die showing it off," Forest said.

"Yeah, man. They don't know what to do with it. They just want money to have. But that green be burning holes in they pockets. Just wasting it."

Jimmee watched as a young-looking man ambled over to the tables they were currently occupying.

He had a large purple bookbag slung over one shoulder. The top was open slightly and he could just make out the tip of a sneaker jutting out of the opening.

Younger-looking guy, he was with a woman that looked a lot older than him. But, like the rest, age came unnaturally to those on the outskirts of life and their mind.

"I don't pay much attention to those kids. They seem not to have even an elementary understanding of self-preservation," Jimmee said adding his two cents to the conversation. Rap had been losing its appeal in the eyes of the general public. Too much death, unoriginality, and an overall feeling of propaganda were associated with the once-pure art form. "Plus I read somewhere something like one or two of them have been dying every month for the past year. Couldn't tell you another industry with a lower retention rate. And, to me, their words aren't about anything. If I'm gonna sign up to die about what I'm saying, at least I'd make it worthwhile. There's far too much happening in the world to only be attentive to base desires. No idea why they just don't let mud fly. Rather have bloody chains."

"Yeah? They're just dumb. I forget you're a writer sometimes, Jim. Fancy way you just dressed up the word stupid," Forest said and took a swig from his Natural Ice right after.

Jimmee laughed.

"It's pretty sad actually," Forest said and wiped his mouth. "Dying for costume jewelry. Clock hitting midnight for a lot of these Cinderfellas."

"That's it. You said the right thing right there. Costume jewelry," Puffy laughed a hearty laugh; slapping the table for extra animation. "Dummies. Doing all that bull jive stuff online just to head to an early grave."

"What's up wit y'all boys?"

The voice came from the young man Jimmee had seen meandering over a few moments before.

"What's up, Snaggle," Forest and Puffy said simultaneously.

"Maintaining," Snaggle said and partially covered his mouth as he spoke.

Snaggle had two front teeth missing and a tooth that projected awkwardly from the side of his mouth which is where he got the Snaggletooth nickname from. He looked to Jimmee to be too young for the hygiene issues he was currently dealing with, but Snaggle and his lady friend were both from the woods. Survival came first.

The older woman with Snaggle remained off to the side. Her head shifted back and forth surveying her surroundings and she was unnervingly jittery for the calm scene underneath the gazebo. Jimmee quietly took all of this in as Snaggle began pulling items out of his bookbag and laying them on the table.

"What'cha got there?" Puffy asked as he peered at everything being laid in front of him.

He had three pairs of sneakers (two were kid's shoes and the other a pair of women's heels), a few kids-sized shirts, 2 windbreaker jackets, a Bluetooth portable speaker, and an electronic digital caliper.

"Got a few new sizes in fellas," Snaggle said and looked up at the men as he finished laying his items neatly across the dusty park table.

"Ah, man. You always got all that small junk," Puff said as he surveyed the clothes. "I can't fit none of the stuff you boosting. You need to start getting some bigger sizes in, Snag."

"Man, get in the gym. I'm not stealing all that big stuff. It'd look like I'm carrying area rugs for the shirt sizes you wear alone."

Forest chuckled at Snaggle's joke. Jimmee did as well.

The woman who walked up with Snaggle suddenly tapped him on the shoulder and pulled him down until her mouth was to his ear.

"I'm bout to go up the hill," she said loud enough for the men at the table to hear.

"What you headed that way for?" He asked looking towards the hill.

A jogger passed the entrance as well as a couple of cars. Wasn't much else happening outside of that.

"Bout to try and find some dog food. I think the DCKHED's scared em' away for a few weeks, but they've stuck to Glory Road for the past few days," she said and looked towards the woods and then back up the hill.

PRIVATE ADMISSION

Jimmee heard this and looked down beside her and Snaggle. He even looked around the park, but for the life of him didn't see a dog. He waited to see if she would repeat her remark.

Forest glanced at her after she made the remark and took another swallow from his beer. He neither looked around nor was he puzzled. He knew exactly what she meant.

Snaggle *woofed* at her and watched as she turned and left before shifting his attention back to his goods he'd spread out like choices at a buffet.

"What's this?" Forest asked as he picked up the digital caliper and slid the digital scale along the attached ruler.

From the looks, it was still new. Out of the wrapper but that's expected when the goods are stolen.

"A ruler," Snaggle said only able to explain with a half-truth. He had no idea about electronics, just knew people paid good money for them. So he always made sure to keep a few along with his other goods.

"I can see that, but what else it do?" Forest asked still studying the caliper.

Snaggle snatched it and studied it momentarily.

"I don't know what kind of ruler it is, but I'm not buying it. Somebody'll buy it though. I'll give it to you for $5 right now if you want it," he said.

"Why would I buy something and don't even know what it's used for?" Forest asked and looked around at the other men at the table.

"That just means it ain't for you then," Snaggle said and placed the scale back on the table. "What y'all up here ta-"

"WHERE MY MONEY YOU SNAGGLE-TOOTHED SNAKE!"

All the men turned their heads towards the woods. Three young men were headed in their direction. Jimmee had seen the boys before and knew they were from the woods. None looked to be over twenty. Young men living old lives. From speaking with them, not prying as not everyone was privy that he was a writer. But just from casual conversation, he had been able to glean that the boys were a combination of runaways and throwaways. The two that had run away had started to live different lives from what they'd been accustomed to growing up. Cognizant of their debauchery, and being of age, they'd decided to tough the world out on their own. An unwise decision that the youth tended to make, especially in postmodern times was that they knew everything about the world they would be inheriting and that they'd be able to survive based on their instincts. Instincts that had not been tested in the wild. And, once they were, the young men were exposed for the juveniles that they were. Especially at such a young age when one is still impressionable. They were the youth that the times were producing. The woods were their haven.

PRIVATE ADMISSION

Even in the distance, Jimmee could make out the subtle bulge in the front of the off-white hoodie the shortest in the bunch was wearing. Just turned seventeen, he'd asked Jimmee for advice about a young lady he was too shy to approach. Jimmee's advice was simple, "Be direct." But it was curious to him how this young virgin gunslinger was so dangerous to the world but still so naive. Death was natural. Love, a mystery.

Snaggle squinted at the group to make out who they were. Realizing what was about to happen, he started to gather his goods back into the bookbag he'd unpacked them from.

"Uh-oh. Them boys headed this way," Forest said.

Snaggle looked once more towards the group that was getting closer to the gazebo.

"I know you hear me Snaggle!" one of the young men hollered as they continued their trek toward the group.

"That's about my time, fellas," Snaggle said stuffing his shoes into the bookbag and zipping it as far as he could. The tip of one of the sneakers jutted out where the zipper stopped.

He was preparing to make a run for it. The men could see what was happening but made no motion to stop the action. No need to be included in the demise of another for their own choices. Free will was a thing. Best to be careful who you owe.

Jimmee saw the young kid reach for his hoodie. He didn't pull anything from it though. Kids. Trying to survive in a cold world.

Snaggle, things gathered, started speed walking towards the hill.

"WHERE YOU GOING SNAG!"

The young kid reaching made a move as though he may chase Snaggle, but he never did. They just continued walking towards the gazebo. They were laughing as they approached.

"That long tooth chump better get my money," one of the young kids said.

He was the leader of the outfit. He was taller than his other two gremlins and seemed the much more outgoing of the bunch.

"What's up wit y'all?"

"I can't call it," Forest said.

"None," Puffy said watching Snaggle reach the top of the hill and continue walking.

"Chilling," Jimmee said looking at the two henchmen.

"One-uh y'all wanna get ya taco ate in Tunk?" One of the henchmen said eyeing the off-brand deck of playing cards on the table.

"I am three times your age young man. Say what?" Forest pressed the young man to explain his slang.

"Pause."

PRIVATE ADMISSION

"That's what I thought," Forest said and sipped his beer.

Everyone laughed.

Just then a twenty-something-looking man walked into the park carrying a young child on his shoulders.

Jimmee took note of the two as they entered, but everyone else at the table was too preoccupied with their own interests to pay any mind.

The pair was closely flanked by what he quickly made out as a worker from the road.

The child laughed that of an innocent; oblivious to the cruelties of the world. His dad twirled him from left to right.

The worker couldn't be bothered with any of it but kept close enough that Jimmee knew they were together.

They made their way past the unawares group and down the path. As they walked, the man made a sharp turn into the woods. The worker followed until none were seen.

Jimmee raised an eyebrow but didn't kick up any dust. The Mickey Mouse conundrum.

He heard the deck ruffle as Puffy shuffled and cut the cards.

"My deal," he said and looked around the table.

Jimmee looked once more towards the woods before throwing the incident out of his mind altogether. Choosing to focus on the card game that was about to begin. These were odds that were more in his control.

CHAPTER V

In Vino Veritas

"I'll be your Huckleberry."

The John was speaking to Muffin who was washing up in the sink. Finished making the beast with her stranger, it was time for her to take a bird bath before fleeing the coop. The door to the bathroom in the rundown motel room was slightly ajar. Her company peered through the crack as they spoke.

"What did you say?" She called out over the running water in the sink.

"I mean I'm up to the task of making you a kept woman," he answered before taking a sip from his glass of whiskey.

She made it clear that she was off-limits emotionally to any of her clients. Only her body felt anything for any of the men. And she wouldn't call what she experienced a *feeling* at all. It was just her body's natural reaction to the physical sensation she was putting it through. Akin to how they tried blaming female victims of unwanted encounters because of the body's natural reaction to pleasure. Albeit forced. One may not want to shed tears after being punched in the face, but that sensation is very real.

"Courting women isn't a chore, Doc. And you'd do best to save all that affection for someone more deserving," Muffin said as she finished wiping her inner thighs.

"Deserve? Silly word. Nobody *deserves* anything. We all deserve death when it comes down to it. Look at me. Good family and a decent job but here I am. On the sketchy side of town with a woman that ain't my wife."

Muffin, finished cleaning up, stepped outside of the bathroom, and finished dressing in plain sight.

Her John watched her as she did so.

"We could do it, ya know?"

"Do what?" Muffin asked becoming slightly annoyed. All men thought they could save a woman it seemed. Even if she wasn't a damsel in distress.

"Disappear. Leave this god-forsaken place and start over. I honestly don't understand your hesitation. What's so good about your work that you won't jump at someone trying to get you out," the man said and gulped the remaining whiskey in his glass.

She resented the question her overzealous partner was now asking. And probably because he was right. *The life* was chaotic. It'd worn on her over time, but she was not romantic about it. She wasn't Julia Roberts and this wasn't *Pretty Woman*. She looked over at the man who was now refilling his glass. He wasn't bad looking, but he was no Richard Gere either. Just some silly man who'd seen too many movies. There had been a couple of prettier and younger tenderoni's that had been fooled by one of these donkeys to leave the life. Mostly, the men would be overcome with jealousy and resentment towards the lifestyles the women could not be bothered to part ways with. Men who couldn't handle a real woman tended to prey on the broken. But she wouldn't claim that title. Not yet.

"What's so good about my work is that it's taught me to see through the desires of naive people who don't know a thing about the real world," she said and walked over and downed the newly poured glass of whiskey.

"Yeah?" her partner said and watched as she wiped her mouth. "And what does something like you know about the real world, pretty lady?"

Muffin set the glass on the nightstand, poured the next round, and sat on the bed beside the man.

"Here you are looking for another somebody. You even said you have a good family. Which means children I'm guessing," she said and looked at the man who winced. "Good means that they're happy. Good even means that you're happy. Yet here you are. Buying more misery than your life can bear. In the real world, something like me uses something like you until the dam breaks," Muffin said.

As if on cue, someone pounded on the door.

"Are you in there, Frank?!"

The voice on the other side of the door was female. Frank's dam had broken.

The man hopped out of bed, rushed into the bathroom, and shut the door with the stealth of a hired hitman.

"Tell her you're here alone," he whispered through the door.

Muffin instantly knew the woman was his wife. She'd dealt with these situations enough during her time that she was neither surprised nor bothered. She stood cooly and made her way to the door. She did a once-over of the room and walked over to Frank's wallet. She took $500 and put the wallet back on the dresser.

She opened the door to see the quaint female on the other side. She was pretty but looked green. The tears welling up in her eyes suggested that she'd be taking him back. That stopped surprising her too. Tears of a clown.

"He's in the bathroom," she said and made her way past the smaller woman. She wasn't expecting a fight or even a shouting match. Women like the one she was now looking at cared more about the embarrassment than the act itself.

The wife pushed past her with no more than a glance in her direction. She stopped short of the bathroom door and turned.

"Hey," she called out to Muffin who turned to look at the woman.

Muffin didn't say anything but raised her eyebrow in a questioning manner.

"Your nose hair is curled up. Did you know?"

♂ ♀ ♂

Grab Yourself Some Gin
The Next Move Will Be A Sin
You'll Never Have More Funk
Than When You're Dancin' Pissy Drunk

Rachel strummed the crude tune on her guitar as she stood on the backside of the 7-eleven. Though there was a bottle of Seagram's Dry Gin sitting on the ground next to her, she sang the song straight enough that the words were understandable. There was a man sitting Indian style on the ground in front of her. He grabbed the bottle, took a swig, and placed it back on the ground near Rachel's feet as she continued her song.

I Can See It In Your Eyes
Behind That Smile The Devil Lies

A song from nowhere that she'd strung together over time. It'd started as nonsensical ramblings on a sunny day on Glory while strumming her guitar to any passerby's on the road, but, after a while, she'd taken a liking to the tune and, slowly, had begun adding lyrics. Sure it came with a sinister twist, but such was life. She sang these last words and bent to

54

pick up the bottle of gin. She took a long gulp before replacing the cap. Rachel set the bottle down, stomped, and strummed her guitar more furiously. The shot had transported her to a time from her youth. When she'd dreamed of making it big as a Rockstar. Before it was trendy to do so and people cared about the music. If only because they'd gotten a chance to express how they truly felt about what was happening in the world around them. Not some escapist visage that only allowed them to play endless love songs about empty romantic pursuits that only led to destruction. That or propaganda shrouded in for-the-people rhetoric that only served to further subvert an already uneducated audience.

"You play good for an old jezebel," the man seated on the ground said.

She wasn't offended. To most that saw her, she was insane. 730 and I don't mean the time of day. An old street siren that cried out to the participants now involved in the age-old profession. Her song was her own.

The man on the ground sitting Indian style was an older gentleman. Down on the ground and down on his luck. He covered his balding scalp with a black skull cap and his hair hung out of the bottom. His camouflage windbreaker was old and dusty and his blue jeans looked just as worn. His black tennis shoes were sitting next to him and his bare feet were neatly folded under his knees. In a third-world country, he may be king. But in this land, where freeman roamed for over 50 years, he was a bum.

"And you look good for an old fool," Rachel retorted.

Muffin stood inside the gas station with a bottle of water and a pack of aspirin. She'd gotten a headache between the walk from the hotel to the gas station. The whiskey played a part, no doubt. Thinking about the man and his wife did help to relieve the pain. If only because she wished he was getting his. So worried about the splinters hanging out of her bum that he couldn't see the 2x4 about to gobsmack him in the face. What a fool he was.

"How much?"

She smelled the beer before she saw his face. The undertone of cigarettes made the lone hair in her nostril shudder.

Muffin swung around and saw the drunken spectacle that had leaned in to whisper his question. Hair unkempt, face ashy, and clothes that suggested he at least made an effort to keep up with the latest fashion, he was a young man. Probably too young for his current inebriated state but the times were cruel.

"What'd you say?" She asked looking at the man.

"I asked how much?" The young man boldly restated his question.

As he did so, two DCKHED PD officers walked into the lightly crowded gas station.

When You Walk That Glory Road

PRIVATE ADMISSION

You'll Find Tales That Are Untold
About The Men And Women Who
Aren't Worth The Gum Stuck To Your Shoe

Rachel was playing her song more furiously than before. The man sitting Indian style on the ground rocked back and forth, eyes closed.

"You deaf? I said how much?"

Muffin turned her attention from the man to the two officers who'd just entered. Chatting with each other, not paying any mind to the happenings around them. The officers walked over to the coffee machines.

"That guy earlier almost popped the cork out of your dam, kid. I'm sure the crowd at the pump enjoyed your show," George said to Christopher.

Like the guilty-hearted(or boastful), they'd returned to the scene of the crime.

"You mean that old Catholic woman? She'll be alright. We didn't shoot anybody."

"Yeah, we got that going for us, for sure. Not much for those news hounds to go off of. No blood, no glory," George said and pulled the lever for the Columbian coffee. Steam rose from his cup as it filled.

"Not right now," Muffin said to the kid who had been staring at her in a daze.

"What'chu mean not right now? I got the money right now," the young man said now beginning to raise his voice.

"Calm down, Scrappy. There's plenty of what you looking for right down that stretch of road," she said motioning towards Glory Road. "Go find you something safe to play with. I'm off the clock."

She fanned him off and turned towards her spot in line. He caught her wrist and stopped her mid-turn.

Christopher, who'd been loosely paying attention, now had a dead stare on the interaction.

"Just be careful before you go rushing into action is all I'm saying," George said and stirred his coffee. "You hear me, kid?"

I Can See It In Your Eyes
Behind That Smile The Devil Lies
So Baby Don't You Fret
This Is One You Won't Forget

"I'm talking to you, Chris," George said purposely to get his attention.

Christopher focused back in on George.

"It's Christopher, sir," he said and peered back over his partner's shoulder.

"Let me go," Muffin said trying to yank herself free. They weren't struggling and he didn't yank her. It was just a man's strength.

PRIVATE ADMISSION

"Come on, ma. Let me try you out."

Muffin looked over towards the coffee at the officers. She and Christopher met eyes. The young man, in his drunken state, was oblivious to their presence.

He began forcibly shoving her towards the door. The other customers in the station now zeroed in on the action, but none moved to intervene. Pillars of salt frozen in time.

Muffin was being inched closer to the door.

"Let me go!" She screamed bloody murder.

Christopher dropped his coffee while George turned his head towards the patrons. Christopher took a step towards Muffin and the young man. George, cooly, placed his hand on Christopher's chest, stopping him dead in his tracks.

"Don't. Let them go," George said seriously.

Christopher, stunned, looked from the door to his partner.

"We can't save everybody," George said and began nudging his partner towards the doughnuts. "Some things you gotta chalk up to natural selection."

Muffin saw George forcing Christopher to retreat and was bemused.

Mouth agape, she wanted to scream, but for who? The patrons in the store had neither the guts nor the patience to deal with other people's matters. Especially if they viewed those issues as avoidable. And this seemed like one of those times.

With one strong thrust, Muffin was shoved out of the door.

CHAPTER VI

Mirrorcle

Muffin had kneed the punk and ran.

She ended up at her favorite watering hole after escaping. In this case, literally. There was a creek near Glory Road. Sugar Creek. You had to know the path to get to it, which kept the locals on the main road, but there were bike paths and an old iron bridge that people could use to cross. There were no driving lanes. You either biked the trail or took a hike.

She didn't frequent the creek but came enough that she was able to find a spot where she could be alone. Especially during the warmer months. It was secluded enough that she could take a dip without worrying about anyone spying on her. Her clients stuck to the road. She wouldn't bring them this way. It was a spot where she could go to forget them for a while. At least enough time to clear her head.

She sat on one of the larger rocks with her feet submerged, twirling a stick in the water. The waterfall near where she was seated was all that she heard besides the constant whistling from the birds.

What was up with those cops? She thought to herself. She had even locked eyes with the younger one. She knew the police and roadies weren't fond of one another, but one was supposed to be on the side of the law that upheld stuff. Maybe they were growing tired of answering the calls from all the sirens on the road.

She shrugged.

A rock plunked into the water near where she was sitting. She watched it sink, and another rock crashed the surface with a *plunk*. She turned to look over her shoulder and saw Jimmee. Jimmee knew about the creek because he was a fisherman. Or that's how he thought of himself. He liked to come out with his pole every few weeks and try his luck. He'd learned how to fish through Youtube videos. The basics at least(mostly how to string his rod properly). He'd caught his first blue gill after hours of fishing the creek. It'd taken him three days altogether before he eventually found the right bait and spot to fish. He was no Bear Grylls, but he took pride in learning new survival skills. Seemed like survival skills was of growing interest to the public.

"What'chu doing down there?" Jimmee called down to Muffin.

PRIVATE ADMISSION

"Came out here to cool off. Heat got people acting different today," Muffin responded and saw Jimmee's notebook tightly clutched in his fist. "You make it down to the park?"

"Yeah. Forest and the boys weren't doing much of anything. Sitting around waiting for the day to end. Snaggle was there."

"I ain't seen him in a while. He stopped coming to the road once he got that new girl."

"He might not be able to show his face anymore. Some of the young boys chased him off not too long after he walked up. Sounds like he owes money," Jimmee said, picked up a small rock, and tossed it into the creek. The small splash made waves, but the water settled quickly.

"Sounds about right. He tried skipping out on a few payments with some of the girls from Glory. Got chased down to the edge of the road by one of the girls. An opportunists if I'd ever seen one."

Jimmee was descending the hill to where Muffin was sitting. There was a lot of overgrown wild grass, Polk grass, and other shrubberies that the city couldn't be bothered to cut back. He watched his steps so he didn't slip or step on an unsuspecting snake.

"Another day in the woods."

"Seen anything worth writing down yet?"

"Not much outside of the normal vaudeville antics. Saw the news van riding up and down Glory but they didn't stop for much outside of lunch. Just need a little more

63

content to get these last few chapters done and I'll be finished with my first book," Jimmee said proudly.

"Famous writer hanging out with the lowly. Got anything about me in there?"

Finally making it to Muffin, he stood and looked as far down the creek as he could. He could see a couple walking across the old iron bridge in the distance. A cyclist zipped past the couple.

"Famous? I don't know about all that. Being famous don't mean much nowadays if it ever did. They're making murderers famous now. But, yeah. A little bit of everything has gone into this story. The exciting and the mundane," he said and looked down to where she was sitting.

"You're using us, ya know Jim. Profiting off our pain."

"And what do you call what you're doing?"

Muffin was silent. Stumped. Without wanting to say it he was right. And she wasn't blind nor would she allow herself to be a sucker for the real world. Yes. She did use her partners. And they used her. But there was an exchange that took place. An understanding. She now looked at Jimmee. The writer. His story was theirs. It felt like an invasion of privacy. Robbery even.

"We understand each other my partners and me. *You*," she said and pointed at him for added effect. "You just take. There is no exchange between us and you. If you did get rich off what's in that notebook, you plan on sharing any of that money?"

PRIVATE ADMISSION

Another cyclist zipped by on the bridge.

"Listen," Jimmee said and hesitated before speaking. "We're all using each other out here. That's just the way it goes. I'm just trying to figure out how to get a better return on my investment."

"Yeah? Well, you ain't investing nothing. What'chu mean get a better return on your investment? Only paper I ever seen you pull out was in that notebook," she said pointing at his composition book.

"You're wrong. I've invested the most important commodity anybody can give."

Muffin waited with bated breath for his response. Jimmee could see he had her on the edge, and, like any good writer, he made her wait.

"And?" she said impatiently motioning for him to continue with his revelation.

"Time," Jimmee responded anticlimactically. "Time is more important than financial gains because you can't get it back. There is no dollar amount on time. Yesterday is done and tomorrow doesn't exist."

He looked back down at her and then down at his side. With the speed of a boxer, he flung the notebook into the creek.

Muffin watched as the current from the waterfall pushed the notebook further down the creek. Jimmee didn't turn his head to see where it went.

"What'd you do that for?" Muffin asked still watching the notebook drift away.

Jimmee shrugged. Truthfully, he wasn't sure why he had tossed his notebook into Sugar Creek. But there was no part of him that regretted that decision.

"Who knows," Jimmee said more to himself than to Muffin.

"You giving up?"

"No. Never. The stuff out here is predictable and I don't know that you're all the way wrong in what you're saying. I think I'll try to find some more interesting stuff to write about. Maybe a little less intrusive if that's even possible. There are more interesting things happening, but nobody cares about that stuff."

She didn't know what he meant but she didn't need to know. She had her own demons to throw in the creek. But she'd keep hers at her side. She made her demons profitable. One man shedding his sins was enough salvation for one day.

Jimmee took off his shoes and submerged his feet in the creek next to Muffin.

"You artist types are weird."

She was the pot and he was the kettle.

"You-"

Hearing the sound of splashing, he turned and saw a family of deer making their way through a shallow portion of the creek. He counted four as they crossed. One of the deer bent down to inspect the notebook. The deer sniffed it a few times before trampling it underfoot and trotting across to catch up to the pack.

PRIVATE ADMISSION

"They say animal senses are stronger than humans. You think they can differentiate stink from perfume?"

Muffin heard the question but had no immediate response. She watched as the flanking deer trotted up the hill and disappeared into the brushes.

"Even if they could, would they care?"

♀ ♂ ♀

"Man, them young guys don't care about much of nothing. For the right price, one of em'll slit yo throat to the other side. They set the expiration date for their own friends. I be trying to talk to em' man. The ones that'll listen anyway. They take it like I'm out here preaching to them and resent what I'm trying to say. I just remember something we called honor amongst thieves. But watching these boys, I ain't so sure if we had honor or we was just lucky. We weren't killers though. At least that's not how we wanted to escape this," Forest said looking around the park.

Jimmee had found his way back to the park. Forest normally stuck around until late in the day. A grown man and one of the more respected men at the park, Forest too was of the woods.

Everyone from earlier was gone. Probably left to stand in front of the little mini-mart not far from the park. The young guys would usually migrate to the store to turn a profit. Until the DCK's came to rain on everyone's sales. And, from what he'd heard from some of the boys, steal the money that they were making.

Jimmee appreciated Forest for his honest talk. He was older, had been through some things, and wasn't shy with information. His daily living was more of a reflection of the society around him, but he had his demons.

In his thirties, Jimmee was younger than Forest but older than the guys from the woods. He understood both sides but leaned more towards Forest. If only because there was too much death happening with the youth and Jimmee couldn't reconcile in his mind the necessity for so many kids dying for nothing.

Even deeper, he wasn't sure if the death was propaganda for more death or just the way the world worked. In his day-to-day he didn't *see* everything being talked about in the news (nor did he make a point to keep up with it), nor could he be bothered with conspiracy theories (there were too many to count, and most sounded like half-cocked theories of why the government couldn't be trusted), but he had a gut feeling that things weren't as they appeared.

"Some of them gon' survive and some ain't. That's just how it's gon' be. My grandma always said fools learn their lesson after they die."

Jimmee had never heard this sentiment and paused to think on it. Forest sipped his beer and waited for Jimmee to digest what he'd just said. He could tell by the look on Jimmee's face that the words resonated with him.

"I'm trying to figure out what that means and I can't," Jimmee said finally.

"Ain't much to figure out. Just hope you don't need death to teach you nothing. Hard to pass on that kinda information, ya know?"

Forest polished his beer, pulled another warm can from his bookbag, cracked it open, and drank deeply before speaking again. Just then he looked down at the path and saw Squirrel cross between the woods. Forest eyed him and shook his head.

"You hear about what happened at the 7-eleven on Glory earlier?"

"No. I've been back and forth today trying to hammer out a story. Must have been something worth mentioning if you're asking. What happened?"

"Squirrel pulled a knife on the DCK's," Forest said and pointed towards the path.

Jimmee glimpsed Squirrel's back as he disappeared deeper into the woods.

"From the woods, Squirrel? That Squirrel?" He asked pointing towards the woods.

"Yep. That's him."

"Why?"

"Plenty reasons out here. Smoked out. Tired. Angry. And honestly, if you haven't noticed, his staircase don't go to the second floor."

Jimmee had seen and spoken to Squirrel on enough occasions, but couldn't say he knew him any more than he knew Forest or any of the boys from the woods. Squirrel sat quietly at the bench for the most part when he did see him.

They played best-of-five on the basketball court sometimes. He came across as a put together guy that was stuck in the Matrix. But he didn't come across as particularly dangerous. Though that's a misnomer. What was the saying? You can catch more flies with honey than vinegar. And hadn't Jim Jones been a likable guy?

"If that's him walking into them woods, I guess they decided not to shoot, eh?"

"Not this time. They jumped him and took the knife. Lucky him. If any of those pigs had bled, he'd be under the jail or another stain on the cement. Yeah. Lucky him alright."

"And they let him go?"

"Looks that way. You saw him walk into those woods just now, right? Catch and release. You know how it go. They waiting for the serious stuff to happen."

"Or just releasing em' so they can commit the serious stuff. Pulling a knife on a cop ain't serious enough?" Jimmee asked with the same irony he heard in Forest's statement.

"Apparently not. Again, lucky him. Never seen a squirrel with 9 lives before."

"Which one you think he on now?"

"10," Forest said and sipped his beer.

And that was about as honest a statement as Forest had made from Jimmee's time spent in the woods. 10. Everybody seemed to be one life past their allotted time.

CHAPTER VII

Brave Prude World

"You. Can't. Say. That."

The child exclaimed before clasping her hands over her mother's mouth. Her mother, lost in her phone conversation and not paying her any mind, directed her stare at the scathing look her daughter was now experimenting with. She slid her daughter's hands slowly away from her mouth revealing her pursed lips.

"Hang on," she said to the person on the other end of the call.

She slapped her across the face much to the shock of the little girl.

"What I tell you about minding grown folks business?" The woman asked her young child and continued with her conversation. She dunked a few of her fries into the ketchup she'd squeezed out onto the hamburger wrapper and stuffed them into her mouth.

Excepting defeat, the young girl folded her arms, lifted and dropped her shoulders like a hydraulic pressing machine in a factory, exhaled an exaggerated, "hmmp" and looked around in embarrassment.

There was a good amount of people in the fast food restaurant, but everyone was focused on themselves. If anyone did see the exchange, they could care less about pressing repercussions.

"That Crypt Keeper can't even ride a bike," her mom said into her cellphone and laughed. She'd cleaned up her previous line, but still managed to get her point across.

The little girl didn't know who or what her mom was referring to, but had been listening to her malign some poor soul for the past half-hour. She was too young to understand adult conversations or their importance. She had just heard her mother using language, in her words, "unbecoming of a young lady" and had decided to correct her.

She turned her attention to the customers in the restaurant and saw a woman with a guitar slung over her shoulder sitting at one of the tables. She studied the woman. Her mom had never brought her to eat on this side of town. The curious people she'd seen since stepping foot out of their mini van was probably a big reason why. But lines at fast food spots were long all over town it seemed. Even though this fast food spot was decently filled, no one was waiting in line.

"Excuse me."

The high pitched voice startled the child. She turned and saw an older female staring at her with crocodile tears welling up in her eyes.

"Did that bad woman hit you?"

The mother and daughter stared at one another.

PRIVATE ADMISSION

"What did you ask my daughter?" The mother said crooning her neck towards the older female and slowly putting down her phone.

The woman ignored the mother completely and focused her attention squarely on the little girl.

"Would you like to come home with me?" The older woman asked the little girl. "You deserve better," she said and held out her arms to the child.

Kicking her in her shin, the young girl hopped from her seat.

"Get away from me granny!" She laughed and ran away.

Her mom watched her and turned her attention back towards the older woman. She nodded a *that serves you right* kinda nod and went back to her conversation.

The tears that were welling up began to roll down her cheeks. She watched as the little girl disappeared around the corner where the registers were and turned her attention back to her mother.

"You don't deserve to call yourself a mother," she said wiping the tears away from her face.

"And you should learn to mind your own business," the mother said half-heartedly. She could care less about the old woman and her feelings.

She wasn't surprised though. This was the new world. Strangers took it upon themselves to butt into other peoples business. Never mind that it may lead unto death if you bothered the right individual. Opinions mattered in the new world. And not in the areas that made much of a difference. Just folks wanting to be heard. She was surprised NEWS 9 wasn't in the shop. This is what led their late night local news stories. People minding each other's business. All while the real issues went undetected, unchallenged, and unforgiving.

The older woman wanted to continue the conflict, but could see that she didn't have a leg to stand on. She looked around. The woman with the guitar slung over her shoulder was the only person paying her any attention.

"Drop it, sugar," Rachel said to the older woman. "You fighting a losing battle anyway."

Rachel was right and she knew it. And though she resented someone with a busted guitar and shabby clothing telling her what to do, there was nothing more she could-

"Well, you can only blame yourself when she ends up with the rest of those people on the road," she had swung her sword one last time.

The comment nicked the young mother.

"Move along, Miss Caryn," the voice came from one of the workers in the restaurant.

She'd known this woman to come in often. They were all privy to her antics and were having none of it. Usually not a bother, but she'd gotten into arguments with a handful of customers. Especially the ones who actually pushed back against her. She had been a missionary from what she'd heard the woman saying on the separate occasions she'd come in to the restaurant. At least she hadn't thrown Holy Water on the woman. Not that it'd happened before, but these types were unpredictable.

"I'm going," the older woman said satisfied that she'd gotten her point across.

She headed for the door and was gone a moment later.

PRIVATE ADMISSION

"Don't pay her any mind. That woman is Planter's nutty. Always bothering somebody."

The mother laughed at the workers comment and looked out the window at the older woman now trekking across the parking lot. She'd pulled a Bible from her purse and was waiving it at the men across the street performing the hand-to-hand motion with the strange men in cars.

"I can see that," she chuckled.

The little girl came back to the table, sat down, grabbed a few fries from her mother's box and shoved them in her mouth.

"Moooom," she said with her mouth full. "Can we leave now?"

♀ ♂ ♀

The pepperoni hit Muffin's face and fell to the pavement.

It was evening. Having left Jimmee at the creek, she'd made up her mind that she wouldn't work the night shift. The day had been treacherous, and she'd already made enough to afford her place to stay and maybe grab some fries from the fast food spot(compliments of the cheating spouse. Walking back down Glory Road, she'd been jumped by the man now pelting her with pepperoni from the slice of pizza he'd been snacking on since stepping out of his black F-350.

"You hear me talking to you?

"I hear you. But obviously you're the one who's deaf. I said no."

He pelted her with another pepperoni.

"Boy. You're annoying. Didn't your mother teach you not to waste your food?"

She didn't always have this nerve. But she learned to be callous towards these strangers. Especially ones like what she was dealing with now. Privileged men who looked down on women like her and couldn't stand to be told no from someone they saw as beneath them.

"Get in the truck," he said but didn't move from his spot.

He could easily overpower Muffin. Even though she was 5'9", he looked to her to be about 6'4".

Probably goes to the gym and eats cauliflower steak too she thought and laughed to herself.

Muffin looked beyond the man further down the road and saw headlights headed in their direction. The man peered over his shoulder and watched the headlights until they passed.

The beige PT' Cruiser crept by. Muffin and Jimmie locked eyes and he continued past.

Must be headed back from Sugar Creek she thought. She wasn't going to flag him down, but she wanted him to stop. He understood her place and never interfered in her business. She, they, were his muse after all.

The man focused his attention back on Muffin.

"If I got to put you in that truck, you're not going to like me very much. I'm asking you to use your own free will and climb in my truck. Or would you rather me drag you inside from that nose hair?" He asked and pointed at her face.

The folly of this life. Any life where the person is for sale. People were always on the market. No matter the day, time, or the hour. When people are for sale. There is no shortage in supply of one's who find power in their secret.

The man looked up when he saw reverse lights headed their way. The beige Pt Cruiser from earlier.

Jimmee reversed into the couple and rolled down his window.

"You look like you can use a ride?" He asked Muffin and winked.

"Why thank you," she said and stepped towards Jimmee's car.

"This is mine, bud. Pick you another flower. I found this one first," the man said and grabbed Muffin's arm.

She pulled her arm free.

"Like I told you earlier, no," Muffin said and kicked him.

His knees buckled inward and he leaned forwards in pain. Jimmee laughed at the look of both surprise and pain every man knows follows the pain Muffin had just inflicted.

"Hopefully that clears your eardrums, sir."

With that, Muffin climbed in the PT Cruiser and Jimmee drove off.

Jimmee pulled into the parking lot of the Inn where Muffin would be staying.

It was close enough to the road that she could get back to work in the morning.

"This is my stop," Muffin said as Jimmee pulled into a parking spot.

"You be safe out here," Jimmee said and looked at Muffin earnestly. "There ain't no supermen out here to save you from all these bad men lurking around."

"Good. I don't need saving anyways. I need *savings*. Coins. Cold. Hard. Cash. You get that right Jimmee? You do know what's going on out here, right?"

"Yeah. I know."

Was all he could think to respond. Wasn't that why he wrote his stories?

"We all gotta eat," Jimmee said.

"But everybody ain't starving."

With that, Muffin tugged on the nose hair until it eventually gave. Jimmee watched her intently. She looked around the inside of the cruiser before snatching Jimmee's hand and placing the hair inside his palm. She curled his hand and looked at him.

"Something to remember me by. Since you threw that notebook in the creek, I'm guessing you won't be out here much. It's grimy out here, Mr. Writer. Much more important stuff to think about."

Muffin climbed out of the car. Jimmee watched until she disappeared into the lobby before pulling off.

78

PRIVATE ADMISSION

The sound of Rachel strumming her guitar rounded out the sounds of traffic in the area.

La Mort Dans Le Mur

(Death In The Wall)
A Short Story

Antonio Robinson

*"Horror and fatality have been stalking abroad in all ages.
Why then give a date to the story I have to tell?"*

Edgar Allan Poe

First things first, my name is Jacob. And I wish I was writing about happier times in my life. People who've made it to my age mostly rekindle the greatest moments they've experienced during their time on the sunny side of the dirt. Especially when their flame is close to winking out. Young people naturally look for a how-to guide in life from their elderly companions. The wisdom of old age is a ruse boys and girls. Gather round.

I've excepted my fate. Sitting here, an old fart at the end of his yarn. Waiting.

As a young man, I worked as a busboy in a retirement community. The work wasn't hard and the workers got along pretty well. My understanding of old age was developed during my time there. Listening to the grumblings of the old heads was upsetting. I've forgotten the

1

name of that retirement home long ago (my mind isn't as sharp as it once was) but I'll never forget the people (or at least their voices). Frivolous rants. Perpetual rants that still call out in my head just before the morning dew dances on a blade of grass in the rising sun, "Why'd they switch the bread baskets!?" and "I hate the new napkin folds!". They were old men and women who'd stored up their wealth for the next generation and had now been taken to pasture. Bags of bones gathered neatly for the Harvester of men. This is what the end meant for those who had earned status during the prime of their lives and held steadfast in unforgiving times that brought strong men to heel. They'd lived only to be locked in a cage. Their zookeepers were their very own children. Every second Sunday of the month was the designated Family Day. We served non-alcoholic wine (which I've always found pointless) and whatever dishes the guest thought up for the chef to toss together in the kitchen. I can still see the cooks grabbing handfuls of corn starch and powdering their nether regions to prevent chaffing during their shift. They'd slide on their gloves right after; washing their hands always seemed to slip their minds.

     In the end, those old men and women were forcing themselves to find ways to retain some semblance of life. Or what they remembered life to be like. Some were pleasant. Others cruel. I didn't mind. I'd clock out and their problems would remain their own. They'd have to climb that ladder alone in the end. Whatever gripes they carried, their feud was never with me. Only that life seemed to not mean much in the end. Like ultimately, all we can do is wait. Much like I'm doing now, I guess. Except, I know what's after me. And maybe it's what's after you too.

LA MORT DANS LE MUR

One thing did come from those experiences; I made up my mind never to have children. I'll leave on my own terms thank you.

I'm writing this to let you know, whoever *you* may be (because in death, one can never know who the probing party in one's life is), It means to take me tonight. I've secluded myself in this one-bedroom apartment (but It's followed me…It *always* follows me) and made my mind up to tell this truth. My truth. The truth of the darkness that lingers under that thin veil of what we know as reality. I've placed electric tape on all the windows (but you know this now don't you) and decided to write this by candlelight. Any light lets It in. Even though the darkness needs no light to see, It needs to know that you see It. Especially at the end.

I think It knows of my intentions to tell my story. I'm sure It does. That thought scares me more than any. That It wants you to know of It and I was the one chosen to pull back the curtain and expose those ones who control what happens in our reality.

But, in my last hours, it's the only thing I've been able to do to get my mind off of my impending…Doom? Damnation? Bliss? Heaven? Hell? Who knows for sure; because those that know are already maggot food. And from what I've learned over the years after lowering a few bodies in the ground, dead men only talk in movies.

I have a few candles. I'll try to keep them going long enough to write. I think I'll finish.

*
**

I grew up during simple times. When life was respected and not rushed by the demands of a callous world. My younger brother Harry and I were children of the South; growing up in Town Innocent, South Carolina. The locals described it as "South til' ya smell it and East til' ya step in it". That smell that they spoke of came from the local paper mill. The second part was more or less a play on the fact that the town sits on the coast and there is indeed plenty of marshland to "step in" as they liked to say. Not a large town at all though. In fact, you could start your favorite song when you entered and drive all the way through before it ended.

Country boys by today's standards. We spent a lot of time at our grandmother's house. Drinking from the spigot after being exhausted from the summer heat, eating from the fruit trees grandma and her siblings had planted when she was a little girl, and experiencing the times in which we lived. Where locking doors and windows were scarce. Nowadays, that'd be a quick way to earn a trip to the morgue. Before the internet, social media and the rest of the abominations that came with the info age replaced the naivety of just being children and the sanctity that came with this. You'd be lucky to get a kid to sit still with all the meds they're pumping into the little buggers now.

Winter or summer, Harry was outdoors. Playing ball on the makeshift goal he had ingeniously nailed to a tree. Or climbing the trees in our yard to examine an abandoned Cardinal or Wren's nest. Harry was like that you see. He'd have grown into a man's man if you know what I mean. He was the craftier of the two of us and was great at doing things with his hands. I may have feigned being an artist in my mind, but Harry was a true artisan.

I was the bookworm. While I was lost in the adventures of some fictional character, Harry was always seeking to create his own adventures. We were different in these ways, but that's what I loved most about my little brother.

LA MORT DANS LE MUR

"You know they got all that junk in those books from the real world, don't you?"

I can still hear him saying this phrase to me whenever he tried dragging me out of the house to join him on one of his adventures. I'd pick the less dangerous (in my mind) adventure to join him on to entertain his sense of wonder. But most times, I'd keep my nose in my books.

"Fine. Just come back to me and report what you find and I'll write about it then."

There was one time he decided that we should go fishing in the canal. There was a path through the woods behind our house, that led the way but neither of us had ever been nor did we have the foggiest idea how to fish. And there was that one kid that drowned in that canal five years before we thought of venturing there alone. Percy. He'd gone with two of his friends that knew how to swim; Percy did not. They'd told him that they could tie a rope around his waist so that he could go in the water and they could pull him back to safety. The local paper reported that the rope came undone not long after Percy jumped in that muddy canal water. No charges were filed. They were kids and they had done what kids do. First and only person I've ever known that drowned. But none of that could stop Harry. And so it wouldn't stop me either.

Wasn't long before we were lost in those woods. In the middle of the day on a Saturday and no sense of direction.

We made it to a clearing and Harry tore his pants on the thorns of a blackberry bush. They seemed to be in every direction we went. The skin underneath the tear bled like he'd been cut with a hot knife and Harry cried muted

5

tears. I stood with him and looked around, trying to figure out what to do. My older brother instincts had kicked in.

The summer heat burned into my forehead as I searched for a sign that pointed us toward home.

Just then the blackberry bushes split into a path. I watched as the bushes parted in a direction I didn't remember traveling to get to where we were standing. Harry, with his head in my chest, didn't see any of this.

I led the way and we went back to safer things. Harry even decided to call it quits for the day. Opting to play inside with his dinosaur collection instead. I never asked him if he remembered how we made it home. But I've never forgotten.

It pains me to write that Harry, the athlete and the adventurer, died while off on one of his quests. Til' this day no one knows what really happened. His partially rotted carcass was discovered after weeks of searching. Now, at this later stage of my life, I'm certain that It had something to do with whatever happened to my little brother in those woods. Grandma used to say, "the darkness knows who It wants." Mostly, I took this as one of her biblical rants she'd get worked up into now and then (mainly while lamenting the high prices at the grocery store), but now I know that the darkness *does* know who It wants.

Harry died several years after It first appeared. Even though he discarded my pleas as something that could only come from the mind of someone who read too much and played far too less, I think he at least wondered if there was any truth in the stories I tried telling him to explain what was happening. I wonder what he'd say about his older brother now. Certified nut. Just like those old fools in that retirement home; afraid of something he's never seen.

LA MORT DANS LE MUR

Hold on. I need to change the candle.

Forgive me. I've digressed into nostalgia. Speaking of Harry does that to me. Some things are good to remember. If only for a moment. But I've never liked romanticism. The story I mean to tell lies ahead.

⁑

I was lost in a horror novel. One of my favorite genres. Maybe this is what It saw? Probably not. But I'd watch all the horror movies I could get my hands on and devour books by the shelf. They were fun really. It was midday (god how certain details never leave) and Harry was outside digging crawdads out of a ditch in the back of grandma's house. At least that's what we called them then. Crawfish is the popular name. We never ate any of the ones Harry caught. He'd just toss them back into the ditch. Although he did experiment by putting one into an ant mound from time to time. I even got a kick out of watching the results. For science. Scouts honor.

Grandma was taking a nap and I was alone in my room (a room that used to house all of my uncles). I had gotten hungry so I got up to grab a snack. When I leapt from the bed, "Hi" was written on the wall. Nothing fancy, nothing deep, just *Hi*. I stood staring at this. I tried to remember whether it could have been there before I'd sat down to read and couldn't. I traced the letters with my index finger.

Dumbfounded, I did the only logical thing I could think of; I walked outside to where my brother was and yelled, "Grandma's gonna get you for writing on her wall!" Hands muddy, Harry dropped the crawdad he was holding and gave me this innocent *I don't know what you're talking about* look. I wasn't convinced and continued nagging him to

7

admit his crimes. He agreed to come in and check out his handiwork. We walked into the bedroom and of course, the message was gone. Not a trace had been left behind. No, "Hi" or any sign of what I was accusing my little brother of doing.

He then scolded me for wasting his time with nonsense. I tried my best to convince him, but with no evidence, my attempts were useless. I even told him about how I traced the letters with my index finger. I traced the word in the exact spot in front of him as if by some stroke of luck I could make the message reappear. Harry watched with childlike annoyance and wonder mixed into one. Nothing happened and without proof, he was having none of it. Smart Phones were decades from being thought of. He turned and went back outside. And I was left holding the bag.

I held a certain pride in being the more responsible, intelligent, and sensible of the two of us. At that point, I didn't care who or *what* had written "Hi" on the wall, I only wanted it to be there. I stood staring at the wall as if trying to conjure up whatever had written this greeting to do so again. If only to prove to myself that I was telling the truth.

Nothing.

I grabbed a snack from the kitchen and, hesitantly, returned to my book. But I never forgot.

A couple yea-

Sorry about that. Wick went out. The darkness comforts me more and more these days. But I'll tolerate the last bit of light I may ever know. Because if I don't tell this before I die, you may never know.

Onward.

LA MORT DANS LE MUR

A couple years passed before the next...showing?
Not sure the proper word, but It came nonetheless. Our
mother had come and taken me and Harry to a
neighborhood twenty minutes from where Grandma lived.

It took a while to get accustomed to my new
surroundings but eventually, I did. Mom even bought Harry
a real basketball goal to help him sharpen his skills.

I had taken to lighter reading. Harry was outside
playing with some buddies he'd made that lived in our new
neighborhood. A wily bunch. They'd all gotten bikes for
Christmas and mostly rode from stop sign to stop sign.

This is when I *SAW*. There was no period of
unawareness and then a sudden awareness. I actually saw
the phrase, "The furnace grows cold Jacob", being written on
the wall.

Frozen, I watched as the message was etched across
my still fresh still white wall.

Remembering what happened the first time, I didn't
rush to tell Harry (and I couldn't blame him this time either)
and mom was at work. She worked in customer service at a
hardware store. She might've got a good laugh before she
hung up on me. And just what would I have told her?
"Mom, um...the walls can talk." This would have been
written off as no more than my imagination.

I wanted to respond, but even at my young age I had
the thought, "How do you talk to a wall?" It never crossed
my mind what may lie beyond.

I'll save you the pleasantries. They mean nothing. I
don't mean to paint the picture of anything human. It. This
thing, in the early stages, only sought to gain my acceptance.
Of what? I can not know. But It did gain my acceptance.
And maybe it was because this was my first friend. My

brother was my brother and I loved him. And to this day I miss him. But I was no good at making friends. This thing came to me. I came not to It. I've been lucky (or unlucky) in this way in my life. My first and only wife was brave enough to approach me. Colleges sought me out. My employers wanted me (nothing huge, but I got by). I've never sought anything. But things, for whatever reason, have always sought me. A gift that has ultimately led to my demise.

    I need to take the candle for a bathroom break. My bladder control has gone the way of my memory; strong at one point, now feeble at best.

Let us continue. Shall we?

    I saw scribbles on the wall. Nothing legible, but there's been nothing legible for a while now. The messages have turned into the scribbling of a child that only wants a parent to know that it does exist. I am here It seems to say these days. And I will quickly bridge the gap.

    This pleasant, if you will, correspondence kept up until I was 24. Harry was now eight years in the grave and grandma twelve. Grandma died of a stroke and Harry, well, go back to the first part of this letter if you've forgotten.

    Two years removed from college and two years from my first, and only wife. I was holed up in a small one-bedroom apartment, not unlike this one. And, yes, these were the years of the retirement community. I mention this age because this is when something strange (if talking to something in a wall isn't strange enough) started to occur. People started dying.

    People have *always* died, right? If this is your argument, far be it from me to force anything against this

LA MORT DANS LE MUR

idea, but the death I speak of is more immediate. I *knew* I had something to do with the bodies that began piling up.

I'd have jobs where I secretly cursed my employers. Unruly customers whose goal in life was to make working-class people miserable. Unsavory individuals overall. At least in my mind. But one by one, they died. Over the course of weeks or months, that person died. Not of anything that would have the authorities suspicious. Well, suspicious of me anyways. Dead is dead. And dead men don't lie.

Thinking about this almost makes me hesitant to pencil this. Almost. But after a few bodies, one starts to notice something. Life sure got easier when the cretins started disappearing. I must admit my guilty pleasure the first couple of times. After all, I didn't touch anyone. Not them anyway.

*
**

My apologies reader. Or maybe I should call you a survivor?

This isn't one of those, "the bad man made me do it," apologies. This isn't an apology at all.

I remember one day that was unlike any encounter I've had with It since. My bones dance when I think of what I saw that day. And more so what I felt.

I was working as a machine operator at a small printing press. The hours were long, but the job wasn't bad. We printed newspapers and books. All local stuff. There were only seven machines in the factory. I can still hear the whiz of those machines when we started them up in the morning. We stayed busy enough that nobody ever kicked up dust about anything serious. Men kept their opinions to themselves to earn their daily bread. That was understood. We all kept our machines running and our mouths shut.

Easiest way to keep your teeth. At least in those days. When there were a lot less sociopaths on the street.

Siblings owned the factory. A brother and sister to be clear. They were both pretty young. More than half of the workers were older. Ken and Karen. Karen preferred to be hands-on. Or at least that's how she viewed her approach to being an owner. To the rest of us, that meant she liked being a pain in the ass (forgive my french). Micro-managing is what the kids call it now I think. Barking unnecessary orders that fell on deaf ears most of the time.

Ken acted as the clean-up crew. He kept the atmosphere light and played mediator between Karen and the rest of us. He'd get into forced pissing contests with the crew when he wanted to flex his knowledge of everything print-related. And whatever investments he and Karen were considering.

I, then and now, found it poor taste to discuss personal wealth with those you pay a pittance. But in the land of the destitute, avarice is king.

I'd stepped away from my machine to take a leak and figured I'd grab a cup of coffee in the break-room before returning to the floor.

"The text on your last batch was crooked."

Karen. I whipped around, splashing coffee on my hand in the process, to see her standing hand-on-hip. Staring at me with a look of disgust she couldn't be bothered to hide.

"What?" I retorted sipping coffee off of my hand.

"Check the alignment on your machine. The text is off."

LA MORT DANS LE MUR

Her way of rushing me back to my station. The text had not been off as I discovered after I'd returned to my machine.

"And learn where your mouth is. How can you expect to print properly when you can't even drink from a cup?" She said before marching back into the factory. Though it was still early in my shift, I was already exhausted from the factory guard dog. Not wanting to finish my coffee, I turned to throw my cup away and there was Ken.

I hadn't heard him enter and Karen made no notion acknowledging that he was in the room before she left. Thinking back, I'd say he appeared more than he entered that break-room.

"The furnace grows cold, Jacob."

The words stole my wind.

There was something that I'm still unable to express. It was a feeling. Like a child feels at the sound of their mother's voice. That feeling (maybe it's an understanding) that the voice knows you.

But how could that devil have escaped from the walls?

Unable to respond, I stared at Ken's face. And It smiled. And Its' smile looked to me, like the smile of someone from another time.

Ken blinked and straightened. I watched as his consciousness rushed into his being.

"Finish that coffee, bud. We need you back on the floor. Words don't print themselves."

He patted my shoulder and exited.

If you're smart, you'll spare yourself from thinking about that encounter any more than you need to. I'm only writing this to escape my nightmares. I'd be cursed for gifting such a burden.

Like a lot of what's happened in my life, I was left holding the bag.

Ken never acknowledged our encounter nor did I press him for an explanation. I assume it's like asking a person if he slept in a crib when he was an infant.

They're us. We're them and they're us.

A line from a movie I haven't seen in years. Probably the most honest phrase I can think of to describe that day.

I couldn't go to the police. I'd have been marked certified 730.

The darkness knows who It wants.

Yeah, right. Wasn't happening. I vaguely remember something my pastor used to say about the power of life and death lying in the tongue. Not sure what passage, or even if it is a passage at all. That's because me and church parted ways long ago. Not that that's stopped It from communicating with me. Religion is man. Nothing more. The darkness. The REAL darkness that exists is something far greater than this. And it *does* know who It wants.

⁂

One candle left. No more digressions. I'll try and finish.

I've always loved magic. Card tricks mostly. I mastered all of the tricks with the Svengali deck. After performing a trick in front of an audience of relatives, I'd frown upon anyone who uttered the phrase, "How'd you do it?" I'd bypass this question with, "Where's the magic in knowing?" This was met with a pat on the head and an, "Alright, kid." Maybe this is why I never questioned when someone died. Even though I had an inkling, the "magic" for me was not knowing.

After I quit work at the retirement home, I took work at a small convenience store. My badge said, "Merchandise Receiving Associate", but in all actuality, that meant that I was a truck unloader. Nothing to be proud of, but it was a check and, more importantly, it limited the amount of contact I needed to have with people. By this time my private life had become just that. I never went out with co-workers and I didn't get into conversations about anything where my opinion would oppose someone else's. I had been isolated in public. Maybe this is what It wanted. To be my only real friend, as unfitting as those words may be.

I met my wife at this store. She spoke to me in the break room and eventually asked me out. It wasn't too long after that we were married. She helped to calm the darkness. My darkness. One has little time to pay attention to walls while making love (god I miss her lovemaking). We never argued (I couldn't allow it!). She died 10 years after we were married of a brain aneurysm. At least this is what doctors termed her death in their medical report. I know better. The darkness *knows*.

After my wife (her name is Candace. did I tell you?) died, I went into depression. People offering their condolences became too much. I moved to another state. I had no one to care for. Mom passed five years into my marriage. Plus, somehow, I thought that It wouldn't follow me. I thought, no hoped that it was confined to that state. That place. Those people

The thought amuses me now. It, They, aren't confined like we are. They know no confines. They know who They want and will stop at nothing.

Antonio Robinson

I worked odd jobs in my new state. I never sought higher employment. Never needed to. I always had enough to get by on. That was just fine with me. The country boy.

The work never lasted long though. As It...They... who knows really? The messages became increasingly aggressive. They began asking me to kill. And I did(you knew that though or you wouldn't be reading this). For what reasons I cannot say. I think now that the killing quieted them. That's what I thought. Now I'm not so sure. Things always go quiet after death. I drowned the manager at my job in my new state. I strangled an employee in my next. But NEVER more than one person in any one place.

I finished the pretty lady across the hall from me. She's in the bathtub (but you know this too, don't you?) Maybe it was the way she smiled at me every day. Always spoke with kind and uplifting words. She even recited a religious quote from time to time when we crossed paths early on Sunday mornings. Those reminded me of home. I always smiled and thanked her but secretly, I wished her gone. What gives others the right to be so damned cheery? Don't they know of the darkness? Surely knowing would drain every ounce of joy from her life. The lives of us all. Knowing how thin that layer between there and here is should terrify even the most brazen men and women.

But they know pain. And she knows pain now too. We'll all know one day.

The candle is almost out and so is my tormenter.

The walls are cracking now, can you see? The red that flows is the blood from a thousand men. Whose I cannot know, but the killing never quieted them. The blood from my sacrifices satisfied them. This is the beast of my creation.

16

LA MORT DANS LE MUR

I can see It crowning-